TASK FORCE DELTA

HOSTAGE CRISIS

Craig Simpson

First published in 2012
by Franklin Watts

Franklin Watts
338 Euston Road
London NW1 3BH

Franklin Watts Australia
Level 17/207 Kent Street
Sydney, NSW 2000

A CIP catalogue record for this book
is available from the British Library.

ISBN: 978 1 4451 0695 3

3 5 7 9 10 8 6 4 2

Printed in Great Britain

Franklin Watts is a division of Hachette Children's Books,
an Hachette UK company.
www.hachette.co.uk

The Real Delta Force

Task Force Delta is inspired by one
of the United States' top-level secret
military units, the 1st Special Forces
Operational Detachment — Delta (1SFOD-D)

also known as

Delta Force

Delta Force's main missions are direct, counter-terrorism
action. They also carry out many secret assignments
including hostage rescues and raids behind enemy lines.

Delta Force (also called "The Unit")
is based at Fort Bragg, Carolina, USA.

Delta Force's motto is:
"Surprise, Speed, Success"

Major Nathan Connor
Highly decorated
Commander of Delta Force.
Transferred from the 75th
Ranger Regiment. Speaks
five languages including
Pashto.

Lieutenant Danny Crow
Second in command.
Came top of his class in Special Forces'
"Operative Training Course".

Lieutenant Jacko Alvarez
A former Navy Seal and
weapons expert.

Sergeant Major Sparks
Comms and intel expert and
veteran of several Special
Forces units before being hand-
picked for Delta Force.

**Master Sergeant
Ben Saunders**
Transferred from 75th
Ranger Regiment. An
expert in survival skills
and demolition.

**Sergeant First Class
Sam Wilson**
World-class sniper skills led to
recruitment into Delta Force,
despite being just 19 (usual
minimum age 21).

CONTENTS

CHAPTER ONE
Hostage grab

Central Afghanistan

The mobile medical station was little more than a sun-baked tent that reeked of antiseptic. Dr Tom Ford said goodbye to his last patient and stepped outside for some air. Within moments he was arguing with a short Afghan soldier called Hajji.

"My orders are to protect you," Hajji insisted. "We must leave."

"There are Taliban all over this goddamn country," Tom snapped angrily. "So what if they might be watching us. Hell, it wouldn't surprise me if half the elders here are Taliban informants. We knew this trip wasn't going to be easy, but the locals need us. We're the only source of medical help for hundreds of miles."

The young Afghan sergeant pointed his rifle towards the steep mountains framing the valley. "Up there are hidden trails to the border with Pakistan. The Taliban use them. They will come in the night and slit our throats."

"Not if you do your job and shoot them first," Tom responded bluntly. "We've only been here a week. We're staying, and that's the end of it."

Dr Kate Shawcross paused to wipe the sweat from her brow and adjust her headscarf. "Everything all right, Tom?" she called out across the dusty, mud-walled village compound.

Tom walked over, pursued by the group of unruly children who seemed to follow him everywhere. "Nothing to worry about. Hajji reckons the Taliban are up in the hills. He probably saw a couple of old goatherders. Told him we're staying. I think he's looking for any excuse to get back to Kandahar." He jerked a thumb towards the Afghan National Army truck where Hajji's two comrades were sitting cross-legged, smoking and sipping tea.

Kate slammed their Land Rover door shut and leaned her back against it. The sun was sinking behind a mountain ridge, turning the barren hillsides a hard blue colour.

"So, how's your first week been?" asked Tom.

"Amazing!" Kate felt exhausted but bursting with pride. "We've reset four broken limbs, amputated a foot, handed out countless antibiotic pills and immunised eighty children against polio. I'd say we've made a difference." She paused thoughtfully. "I don't like the way the locals gawp at me, though. And they didn't

7

exactly welcome me when we arrived."

"It's not that they're ungrateful, Kate. They just don't think women should do this work."

"I know, but even so—"

A sudden shout for help made both Tom and Kate turn in alarm. They saw a tall, skinny man hurrying along the village track. It was littered with stones and potholes. He was carrying a boy in his arms. The boy's shirt was soaked with blood.

"Quick, Tom," said Kate, reaching for the vehicle's door handle. "Give him a hand. I'll grab the medical bag."

Hajji's men rose slowly to their feet.

"*Komak! Dakter!*" the man carrying the boy called out breathlessly. "Help...Doctor. Please."

Kate swung the bag over her shoulder and shouted, "Hajji, come on. We may need you to interpret for us."

Tom reached the boy first. His body was lifeless. Tom helped to gently lower the boy to the ground. "Who are you? What happened to him?" he asked the tall, bearded man dressed in pale baggy trousers and a loose-fitting shirt.

"*Assalam u alaikum* — peace be upon you. His name is Hassan. He fell down a mountain. I am Amin and brought him to you so you can save him, *inshallah*."

Kate arrived with Hajji close behind.

"Pass the surgical scissors, Kate."

Carefully, Tom began cutting away the boy's shirt. "He's lost a hell of a lot of blood. Grab some pressure pads. We need to slow down the bleeding."

Gently, Tom peeled back Hassan's shirt. "What the hell?" He froze in astonishment. There was no wound.

By the time they heard the incoming rocket-propelled grenade it was too late. Hajji's army truck exploded into a ball of flames. Shrapnel cut down Hajji's men, hot fragments slicing through their uniforms. Tom sprawled flat on his stomach, covering his head with his hands. Kate shielded the boy as debris fell around them, peppering the ground. Cracks of rifle fire echoed around the houses, each shot making Kate flinch with fright. She thought she heard Hajji shout something but didn't dare raise her head.

Silence. "Tom, are you OK?" Kate couldn't conceal the tremble in her voice.

"Yes. Are you?"

"Uh-huh." Kate turned her head. Her ears rang from the blast. She gazed at the burning remains of the truck. Bodies littered the ground.

From doorways and rooftops, and from gaps in the compound's mud-brick walls, Taliban fighters emerged. Kate sat up and saw Hajji lying next to her, his throat cut. She shrieked and looked up at the figure standing over her. Amin — the man who had carried the boy to them — held a knife in his hand, its blade was covered in blood. Confused, she looked down at the boy.

Hassan opened his eyes and leaped to his feet.

As Tom tried to stand, Amin grabbed him

around his neck and held the knife against his throat. "Don't move, infidel."

In seconds, Kate and Tom were surrounded by Taliban fighters. Some carried heavy machine guns and ammo belts, others were just wearing trainers and dressed in dusty *pirhan tonban*. A man pressed through the circle and grinned toothlessly. He was the Taliban leader, Masud. "Well done, young Hassan."

Hassan tore off his tattered shirt in disgust. It smelled horrible, and felt cold and clammy against his skin; Masud had used goat's blood.

Amid chants of *Allahu Akbar* Masud issued orders to his men. "Gather weapons and strip the jeep of anything useful." He pointed at Kate. "You will come with us. Amin, tie her hands." He then turned to Tom. "You, infidel, will return to Kandahar with a message. Here, give this to the American general." He pressed a piece of paper into Tom's hand. "These are my demands. One million dollars if you want to see the woman again, alive."

"Take me instead," Tom pleaded. "Let her go."

Masud shook his head. "She is worth ten times more than you. We know she is the daughter of an American senator. Tell the general he has one week, or she will die."

CHAPTER TWO
Taliban trap

Central Afghanistan

The following day and several hundred miles further north, Major Nathan Connor and his Delta Force team were on a reconnaissance mission. They were driving to a new hydroelectric plant and dam. A mile behind them was the main convoy, which included a small party of American politicians and the head of Central Command, General Patterson.

Taking point duty, Delta Force opted for their Ranger Ground Mobility Vehicle. The GMV was a version of the Humvee stripped of its doors to enable instant access and use of small arms from inside. Connor had a grenade launcher mounted on top, as well as a heavy machine gun. He was confident they would be able to handle Taliban resistance. Plus there were two Black Hawk helicopters circling above the main convoy. Just as long as the track is clear of IEDs, we should be OK, Connor thought.

The road was dusty and heavily rutted. Sergeant Sam Wilson was at the wheel of the

GMV next to Connor. Sam pulled the GMV off the main track, up a steep climb. The road wound in a series of tight bends towards the dam. Connor felt a tap on his shoulder. "What's up, Sparks?"

"CENTCOM says they've lost contact with the dam construction site, sir. Visual feeds from high altitude drones have detected suspicious movement on the mountainside above us."

"Right. Try to call the site staff yourself, and inform General Patterson. In the meantime,

I guess we'd better check it out. Sam, put your foot down."

As they approached, Connor ordered Sam to pull over. Dozens of temporary buildings — home to the construction workers and their families — had created a small town. They overlooked the half-built dam on both sides of the road. The site office was located at the far end of the street.

"Sparks, any luck raising the site staff?"

"No, sir."

"OK, we'll do a recce on foot. Sam, you stay here and establish a line of fire to the rocks above us. Ben, you're up top. Danny and Jacko, come with me."

Connor grabbed his M4 rifle and jumped out. Lieutenants Danny Crow and Jacko Alvarez ran to take up tactical positions on either side of the road. Connor walked, his eyes darting from doorway to doorway. He checked the flat rooftops and alleyways, but the place appeared to be deserted. The only thing he could hear was the thud and hammering of construction traffic in the valley beyond. After twenty metres he stopped and knelt down. He waved Jacko forward, and signalled for Danny to move up.

"It seems OK, sir. Sounds like everyone's at work on the dam."

"Perhaps." Hearing an approaching Black Hawk, Connor realised the VIPs would soon arrive. "Let's get a move on and check out the site office."

The site office was a grey Portakabin at the entrance to a large, wire-fenced compound protecting heavy machinery and materials. The door was open. As Connor approached he called out. There was no reply.

He pressed up against the wall next to the door, counted to three and then spun round into the doorway, M4 raised and finger on the trigger. A fan whirred noisily, fluttering piles of paperwork. Connor saw a body on the floor behind the desk. Blood was splattered on the wall. Then he saw the large package and a mass of coloured wires. He turned quickly. "Fall back to the GMV, now! This place is rigged to blow."

They hurried along the street towards their GMV. Connor spoke into his helmet mic, telling Sparks to warn the convoy to abort the visit. The sergeant's reply made Connor's guts tighten.

"They're already here, sir."

"Then tell them to take up defensive positions and hold. The bomb might be detonated remotely by Taliban as soon as the VIPs are in range."

A boy leaned out of a window in one of the temporary houses. He waved and pointed to a house opposite. "Boom! Boom! *D kor deneneh!*" he yelled, before ducking back inside.

Connor's instinct kicked in. The boy was telling him that there was another bomb inside the house. They were in the middle of a Taliban trap!

"Prepare for incoming," he warned his team. Had the convoy reached the site office and the bombs been detonated, there'd be no evac route — no way out.

Gunshots cracked from the hillside above. Danny let out a cry and sank to his knees. Connor grabbed Danny's webbing and began to drag him back towards the GMV. Jacko covered their backs, laying down a blanket of covering fire.

"Danny is hit," Connor announced into his helmet mic. "Ben, there's a second bomb in that house I've just passed. Hit it with everything you've got. Sparks, there are snipers up on the hillside. Call in our Hawks to take them out."

"Roger that, sir."

Connor hauled Danny to the cover of the armoured GMV. Coughing between gasps for breath, he managed to speak, "I'm OK, sir. Body armour did its job. Just winded me."

Next to them, Sam steadied his aim. He had a target in the crosshairs of his rifle sight: a figure crouching behind a rock some five hundred metres away. Sam exhaled, gently squeezed the trigger, and absorbed the recoil. "That's two down, sir, but there are at least five more of them up there."

The pair of Black Hawks screamed overhead, and fired rockets at the hillside, turning it into a dust-laden fireball.

"Not any more, there aren't," Sparks added with immense satisfaction.

Grenades pumped from Delta Force's GMV launcher, blasting the house where the boy had been. "Jesus, cease firing, Ben! Cease fire! That's the wrong house!" Connor shouted.

He grabbed the trauma kit from the GMV. "Sam, cover me!" he ordered, and then hurried back along the street to the remains of the house. Connor searched through the debris until he found the body of a woman. He checked for a pulse. There wasn't one.

Jacko arrived in support. "Marines from the convoy are locking this place down, sir. Sparks has called in an anti-IED team to check for other bombs, but they won't be here for at least an hour."

"Shut up!" Connor snapped. "Listen." He could hear faint cries. The boy was there, somewhere, and was still alive. "Over here. Quickly. Give me

a hand lifting this wood panel."

The boy, covered in yellow-grey dust, was in bad shape, his left leg crushed just below the knee. His piercing screams rang in Connor's ears. After a quick check, Connor knew he had to stop the blood surging from the crushed leg. He applied a tourniquet, while Jacko pushed a fentanyl lollipop into the boy's mouth to dull the pain. Over his cries, Connor was only vaguely aware of voices and footsteps behind him.

"Senator Shawcross, it really isn't wise to be out in the open. Please return to your vehicle, where you'll be safe," General Patterson called out. "I must insist."

"Nonsense, that boy needs my help. I was a doctor for twenty years before entering politics."

Rolling up his shirtsleeves, the senator stooped down beside Connor. "Well done, soldier, but that tourniquet needs to be even tighter. Here, let me do it. We must get this boy to hospital within the hour."

"Impossible," General Patterson replied. "It's over two hours back to Camp Delta by road."

The senator studied the circling Black Hawks for a moment before searching the local terrain. He pointed, "Over there. Get the pilot to land and take the boy back to Camp Delta."

The boy cried out for his mother in his native Pashto, *"Mor! Mor!"* Connor held him and whispered that everything was going to be all right. He thought of his own son back home, and the hit and run accident that had cut his life so short. And he thought of Hassan, the son of his childhood friend, Assif, and the promise he'd made to find him. A promise yet to be fulfilled.

As the Black Hawk took off with the boy on board, General Patterson received an urgent and disturbing message from CENTCOM. Grim-faced, he broke the terrible news to Senator Shawcross.

"Senator, the Taliban have attacked the medical station where your daughter was working. She's been taken hostage."

CHAPTER THREE
Mountain path

Southern Afghanistan

Kate pressed her eyes shut tightly. She couldn't bear to look down. The high mountain path was narrow and the long drop down into the valley below made her feel dizzy. With her hands tied, she found it difficult to balance. One wrong step and she'd fall.

Kate was hungry, thirsty and stank with stale sweat. She was terrified, but determined not to let it show — not to give her captors the satisfaction. Her left foot suddenly slipped and she let out a shriek. Loose stones tumbled down over the edge.

Hassan appeared at her side. "Take my hand. Surely, you're not more afraid than a stupid goat? See how they climb without a care."

Kate had noticed the goats dotted about the steep mountain side, grazing quietly. They did little to reassure her. "Your English is very good. But a goat has four legs. I've only got two."

The Taliban leader, Masud, overheard and before Hassan could reply, snapped, "Then crawl on your hands and knees, woman."

"Damn it, I wish I'd never set foot in this hell-
hole. I only wanted to help, and this is the thanks
I get. My feet are sore and my head hurts. How
much further is it?"

Hassan looked away and felt choked. He had
regrets too. All he had wanted was to find the
Taliban camp and then tell the Americans so
they could come and avenge his father's murder.
Setting off after Masud had been his first big
mistake. Getting caught by Masud was his second.
Worse, he'd lied to the Taliban leader about
wanting to join their jihad, their holy war against
the American infidel. It was a lie that Hassan
feared would bring him a great deal of trouble.
Already, Masud had used him. Hassan hated the

fact he'd played a part in Kate's capture.

Amin, the tall young Taliban fighter who had carried Hassan to the medical station, caught them up. He handed Hassan a bottle of water. Hassan had grown to like Amin because he seemed different from the others, with his constant joking, *tanbūr* playing, and fine storytelling around their campfires.

"Masud's in a really bad mood today," Hassan observed.

Amin nodded. "His shoulder wound is painful and he is still angry about the American infidels' attack we suffered a few weeks ago. We lost many good men, not to mention the drone and its missile intended for the American President's visit. Still, we are used to setbacks. That is our story, the story of our country, Hassan. Our struggle is a hard one, harder even than trying to empty an ocean by throwing stones into it. We need to regroup and begin again. Taking the woman hostage was an opportunity not to be missed."

An old man with a long grey beard emerged from behind a boulder, waved his stick in the air and called out. Masud approached the goatherder and spoke to him. Hassan took the opportunity to rest. He sat down, groaning at his

24

aching muscles. He counted the blisters on the soles of his feet. Amin settled down cross-legged next to him.

"Do you think he's warning us of trouble ahead?" Hassan asked.

Amin shrugged. "Perhaps. This is dangerous tribal territory. The Baloch warlords are always switching sides. One week they welcome us with open arms, the next they'd happily cut off our heads." He sighed. "The sooner we reach our training camp close to the border with Pakistan, the better. We have dependable friends there."

"Do you think the Americans will try to rescue her, Amin?"

"Perhaps." He gestured to the mountains. "This is mujahedin country, Hassan. There are many hidden caves and crevices. Men can vanish in the blink of an eye. It will not be easy for them to catch us."

Hassan shivered. Amin and the others considered him one of them now, a Taliban fighter. Plagued by guilt, he recalled how his father had despised the Taliban. As they set off once again, Hassan made a silent promise to himself. When the time came he would escape and, so the world would know he was no Taliban fighter, he'd rescue Kate too.

CHAPTER FOUR
GPS tracking

Ops Room, Camp Delta

"Official US policy is an ass!" Senator Shawcross shouted, banging his fist on the table. "We're talking about my daughter. If a million bucks is what it takes, then so be it."

General Patterson tried to calm the senator. "Paying a ransom is no guarantee we'll get Miss Shawcross back. And any rescue attempt will need careful planning—"

"You heard what Dr Tom Ford said. We've got a week." The senator pointed to a large map on the wall. "That region's huge, and right now she could be anywhere, goddamnit."

"Our sources on the ground say they're heading for a remote compound close to the border, where we believe there's a Taliban training camp. We've been gathering intel on it for some time now," the general added.

"Well, why don't you go after them and kick some butt?" the senator snarled angrily.

Connor was sitting at the back of the room but only half listening. He was studying Tom Ford's debriefing notes and a copy of the ransom demand. Tom's description of the Taliban leader at the medical station fitted Masud right down to his toothless grin. Connor's thoughts then turned to his personal mission to find his late friend's son, Hassan. The two were linked. Finding Masud would also mean locating Hassan. During a previous mission to destroy a US Predator drone stolen by Masud, Connor had found evidence that Hassan was among them.

The general drew the meeting to a close and a frustrated Senator Shawcross was shown out.

Connor stood. "Now the senator has left, can you fill me in on what we do know, General?"

"Of course, Major. We're tracking Masud and Miss Shawcross' precise movements. Miss Shawcross has a personal GPS tracker. It was issued to her before she left Kandahar. Provided she keeps wearing it we'll always know where she is, down to the nearest metre or so."

The GPS would lead them right to Hassan, too, Connor thought. He could scarcely hide his delight. "We'll be attempting a rescue, I assume."

The general nodded. "Joint Ops is putting together detailed plans."

"I want in, sir."

CHAPTER FIVE
Masud's injury

Southern Afghanistan

In a cave somewhere in the mountains, Hassan sat next to Kate Shawcross watching goat stew bubbling slowly on a fire. Hassan hated goat stew. Instead, he had trapped a wild hamster, killed and skinned it just as his father had taught him.

It had roasted over the fire during evening prayers, and now he pulled juicy flesh from the tiny bones. He offered some to Kate.

"Gah! Are you kidding?" Kate scrunched her face up and looked away.

"It is rude to refuse," Hassan replied in English.

"Yeah? Well, I'd say kidnapping is a far worse crime. How old are you, anyway?"

"Twelve," he replied. He sat down next to her. "In our country," he continued, "we always treat guests, even our enemies, with respect. That is our way, the Afghan way."

"Really? Well, thanks, but no thanks."

Orange flames flickered and danced on the wall of the cave. Amin sat cross-legged close to the fire plucking tunes on his *tanbūr*, a long-necked lute.

Hassan shuffled a little to his right, pressing up close to Kate. She leaned away. "I am a prisoner too," he whispered. "I had no choice but to join them. The Taliban killed my family for talking to you Americans. I am waiting for my chance to escape. I can help you. When the moment comes, we shall get away together."

Kate stared at Hassan, open-mouthed.

Masud was in deep conversation with some of his men. Kate noticed he was perspiring heavily, shivering and looking exhausted. Fresh blood seeped through his shirt from his old shoulder wound. "How much further do we have to go?" she asked Hassan.

"Amin tells me another three days or so before we reach the Taliban training camp close to the border. Why?"

"Oh, just wondering." Kate's medical training told her that Masud was sick. Very sick. And that scared her. She could tell the others depended on his leadership. Without it, she feared the worst possible fate; that they'd abandon their hostage plan and simply kill her. Would ISAF try to rescue her? Would they come in time? Kate reached up to make sure the top buttons on her blouse remained fastened. Beneath, hung round her neck, lay a chunky necklace containing a GPS tracking device. The local ISAF commander had insisted she wear it. Thank god, she thought. At least they know where I am.

Mid-sentence Masud closed his eyes and slumped over.

"Masud! Masud!" Those beside him panicked, jumping to their feet, shouting, pulling at his arms to try to get him up. Someone called out, "I think he's dead!"

CHAPTER SIX
Connor has a plan

Camp Delta

Connor was ordered to attend the late-night official briefing together with the commanders of two other Special Forces units, Arrow and Spear.

"Trying to take on Masud in the open is simply too risky, and so we're going to let him reach their training camp," the head of Joint Operations announced. "It'll mean taking on more Taliban, but we judge the odds will be in our favour. Using the GPS tracker we'll know Miss Shawcross's exact location and so the extraction team can be in and out fast. Major Connor, I'd like your Delta Force team to handle that."

Connor nodded.

"Meanwhile, the compound will come under sustained assault from Arrow and Spear in a manner that will maximise confusion and mayhem. Speed and surprise will be crucial. Once Miss Shawcross is clear, co-ordinated air strikes will obliterate the camp."

Connor sat up with a jolt. He knew from satellite photographs that the camp was large and realised that he'd have precious little time to seek out Hassan as well as rescuing Kate. "Sir," he called out. "We must surely attempt to capture everyone alive. They will have useful intel for us."

"Normally, yes, Major. On this occasion, however, it has been decided to go in hard."

Connor's mind was in turmoil. How would he find Hassan in time?

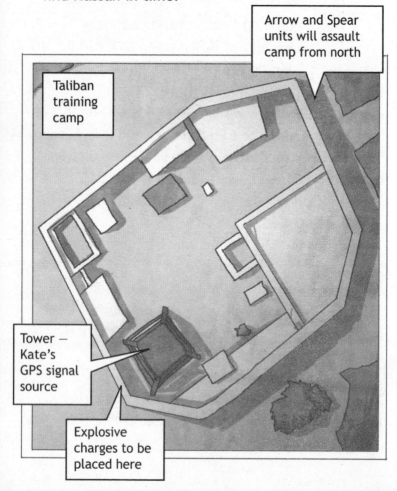

Arrow and Spear units will assault camp from north

Taliban training camp

Tower — Kate's GPS signal source

Explosive charges to be placed here

After the briefing was over, Connor paid a visit to Camp Delta's hospital. He sat for an hour beside the bed of the injured boy from the construction site. The constant bleeping of the machines told him the boy was stable, and he'd overheard the surgeon say he was expected to make a full recovery, even though he'd lost a leg.

But as he sat there a plan was taking shape in his head. It was a plan he supposed Central Command would never agree to because it carried huge risks. Hassan wasn't a priority for them, but Connor couldn't leave him behind.

He took out his cell phone and scrolled down to the number of a local "fixer" he'd had many dealings with, and could trust.

"Abdul, Major Connor here. *Assalam u alaikum*. Listen, I need a big favour. Do you know a Baloch warlord by the name of Faruq? He lives close to the Pakistan border."

"*Wa alaikum u ssalam*, Major. Yes, I know him."

"Good. I've met him a few times. He tolerates the Taliban but has no love of them. They have a training camp in his area, and I need to get inside undetected. I figure the only way is by being among faces familiar to the Taliban there. My question is: can Faruq get me in?"

"It may be possible. I shall call him for you,"

33

Abdul hesitated, "but, it will be expensive."

"There's five K in it for you, Abdul, and offer Faruq as much cash or as many camels as it takes. Just no weapons. Understood?"

"Yes, Major. I will offer horses. Faruq loves horses. A fine stallion would make him the envy of all the local warlords."

"Fine. But this is urgent, Abdul. I need an answer within twenty-four hours."

"I shall do my best. But a word of warning, Major. I know Faruq has worked for you Americans in the past, but his loyalty is as unpredictable as the wind. He cannot be entirely trusted."

Connor put his phone back in his pocket and stared at the bleeping heart monitor. Now, provided Abdul delivered, he just needed to convince his men that his plan could work. If all went well they'd be heroes. If not, they'd either be court-martialled or dead.

CHAPTER SEVEN
Kate saves Masud

Southern Afghanistan

Inside the cave, it took three of Masud's men to restrain Kate.

"He's still breathing. I'm a doctor for chrissake. Unless you let me help him, he will die."

"No...no...you are a woman. It is not permitted."

Hassan had an idea. "Amin and I will help. She can tell us what to do. That way she does not have to lay hands on him."

Reluctantly, the others let go of Kate. "Hassan, grab the medical bag the others took from me. Amin, carefully remove Masud's shirt. I need to look at that shoulder."

It was as Kate suspected. The wound was infected and she reckoned the bullet was still lodged deep in the muscle. "Right, we must clean the wound. We'll give him some antibiotics too, but there's a problem. That bullet has to be removed."

"What? Here? Now?" Amin asked.

"Yes, here and now. Either you let me cut it out, or I'll show you how. Which is it to be?"

Amin looked up at her. "And that will save him?"

"It's our best shot."

Amin swallowed hard. "Then show me how, and may Allah bless me with a steady hand."

With Masud sedated, Amin took a deep breath and pressed the scalpel into his flesh. Blood and yellow pus oozed out. Kate watched closely. "Cut deeper into the muscle," she said. "Much deeper. And stop shaking."

Beads of sweat formed on Amin's furrowed brow and trickled down, dripping from the end of his nose. Eventually, he felt the scalpel touch something solid. "Quick, Hassan, hand me the other tool."

Hassan hurriedly passed the tweezers to Amin and held his breath. Carefully, his friend began to pull out the bullet.

"Allah be praised!" Amin said as he dropped the bullet into Hassan's palm.

The operation was complete, and Amin needed some fresh air. He wandered outside the cave, with Hassan close behind. Kate stayed by the fire and tried to get some rest.

"This is all wrong," Hassan whispered to Amin. "Kate is a good person. We must let her go. No enemy of the Taliban would help save Masud."

Amin said nothing.

"My father used to tell me stories about his

best friend when he was my age. An American boy called Nathan Connor. Nathan's father was a doctor too, and saved many Afghan lives, including my grandmother's. Masud is wrong. Not all Americans are bad."

Lifting his head, Amin gazed up at the stars. "It is more complicated than that."

"No it isn't," Hassan protested. "All they want is to bring freedom and peace to our country. To make our lives better."

Amin turned and looked at him. "The infidels do not share our beliefs. They want to impose their will upon us. This is our country, Hassan, and they are not welcome here. They must go home or die. It is their choice. Do you think they would act any differently to us if the tables were turned?"

"No, but not everyone sees things the Taliban way. Our country is home to many different peoples like the Pashtuns, Tajiks, Uzbecks, Turkmen and Baloch. Some are Sunni Muslims, others are Shi'a, and they are always arguing. If the Americans go, they will all be at one another's throats again, worse even than now. There will be no peace or freedom."

Amin laughed then sighed. "Perhaps you are right. But now we must sleep."

CHAPTER EIGHT
Amin's story

Weak and feverish, Masud could not walk far unaided. For three days his men took it in turns to carry him and it slowed their progress.

Kate tried to walk as slowly as possible too, frequently demanding they stop to rest. She thought that the longer it took them to reach the training camp, the better the chances were that a rescue attempt would be made. As she walked she studied the ridges and valleys, and listened out, hoping to see or hear her saviours come. But they didn't, and she began to wonder whether the tracking device around her neck actually worked.

"I still think we should let her go," Hassan said to Amin.

"If it were up to me, I'd let her go, Hassan. Just to shut you up! But, I have spoken to Masud and it's out of the question. He is grateful, of course, but insists it changes nothing."

Hassan caught Kate staring at him and supposed she was relying on him to mastermind their escape. Any idea of sneaking off in the middle of the night was hopeless — Kate was closely guarded at all times. "Can I ask you something?" Hassan said as they paused to rest on a high ridge between two valleys. Amin nodded wearily. "What made you join the Taliban?"

"My home town of Kalat was bombed. All my family killed. The Americans initially denied it, but eventually said that it was a mistake. Their intelligence was wrong. So, you see, Hassan, we share much in common. Both our families, both our innocent fathers and mothers are dead."

Hassan despaired. What Amin said was only half true. The big difference was that it had been the Taliban who'd killed Hassan's family, not the Americans. He suddenly felt the gulf between them widen to that of a great ocean, but he still wanted to think of Amin as a friend.

"So, I chose jihad," Amin added. Shielding his eyes he scanned the valley below and then reached out and pointed with delight. "Allah be praised. There is the camp, Hassan. See it? With good fortune we shall reach it by dusk. Go and pass on the good news to the others."

Hassan could just make out the mud-brick walls that formed the perimeter of the camp. There were buildings too, including flat-roofed towers at each corner. He got up and wandered back to where Kate was sitting. "We shall be there by nightfall," he said, noticing the growing fear in Kate's eyes.

CHAPTER NINE
The mission

Camp Delta

Connor had heard back from Abdul that Faruq was willing to help him. He'd also had confirmation from Central Command that Masud and his men had reached the training camp. Connor rounded up his Delta Force team for a briefing.

"The GPS signal indicates Miss Shawcross is being held in the tower at the south-west corner of the compound. Central Command's plan is as follows. Units Arrow and Spear will helo in to the north, head south and launch an assault. Zero hour is tomorrow at midnight. The moment they engage the enemy we will blow a hole in the compound's perimeter wall close to the tower. We extract Miss Shawcross and get the hell out of there before the air strike. Naturally, this means that before everything kicks off, we have to get to the wall and place the explosive charges undetected."

Connor was surprised by the silence. Finally, Ben piped up. "OK, sir, maybe you'd now like to tell us *your* plan."

Sparks added, "We know you're still looking for the boy, Hassan. And he's probably there too, with Masud, right?"

Connor was stunned. "You guys don't miss a thing."

The team smiled. "We can read you like a book!" Sparks laughed.

"All right. This is what I have in mind. We're going to rendezvous with a local Baloch warlord called Faruq." Connor saw the surprise on the faces of his men. "Bear with me, guys. At my request, Faruq has called a shura, a meeting with the training camp's leaders, to discuss some issues. Apparently, the latest group of Taliban recruits has been stealing his chickens and he's not very happy about it. I'm going with him. I'll find Hassan and then get to Miss Shawcross by the time you're set to blow the wall."

Ben whistled through his teeth. "Can you really trust this Faruq? And what if you get caught? We'll lose the element of surprise."

Sparks came to Connor's defence. "That's true, but Major Connor can make an excellent case for being on the inside. Our blanket charges will blow one hell of a hole in that wall and will cause substantial damage to nearby buildings. If Miss Shawcross is standing in the wrong place at the wrong time we may end up dragging out her dead body. It would be far better if someone was there to make sure she's safe."

"And don't worry about Faruq," Connor added. "He's getting everything he wants. Ten of the finest horses in this region of Afghanistan. I've bought his loyalty."

Sparks looked round for nods from the rest of the team and then said, "OK, count us in."

"Just one question, sir," said Sam. "Why ten horses?"

"Four will carry our supplies. The rest we ride to meet up in secret with Faruq, at the entrance to a mountain pass west of his camp. We'll fly in and pick up the horses. We'll have just a three-hour ride ahead of us."

CHAPTER TEN
Fate of the hostage

Taliban training camp, Afghanistan / Pakistan border

The following day, Hassan was told to join a group of new recruits. His time was filled with prayers, exercise, weapons training and instruction on tactics for guerrilla warfare.

He barely had a moment to himself, but Hassan still felt lonely, fearful and out of place. A strange atmosphere hung over the camp. When they were shown the row of suicide vests and ordered to try them on for size, he felt the desperate urge to run away. The others put them on, and were keen to learn how they should best detonate them in crowded places. All Hassan could think of was escaping.

Finally, he had the chance to talk to Amin. His friend looked far from happy.

"The camp's leader has taken my *tanbūr*," Amin complained. "Music is not permitted here. What is life without music?"

"That's a shame. How is Masud?" Hassan asked.

"He's resting."

"The Americans have one more day to fulfil his

demands. Allah willing, they will pay the ransom. Then Masud can release Kate." Hassan noticed that Amin looked away. "What? What is it?"

"I fear Kate's fate is already sealed."

"What do you mean?" asked Hassan anxiously.

"I overheard them talking, Hassan. The camp's leader is very angry that Masud brought her here. He fears that the Americans might attack. Worse, he said that as she knows our location, she can never be freed. They will kill her, whatever happens."

"They can't. We must do something, Amin."

"There is nothing we can do, Hassan. Now, I have to go. I have been given a dozen tasks. Tomorrow evening there is an important shura here, a meeting with a powerful local Baloch warlord."

Hassan sat well away from the others in the camp and desperately tried to think. Kate's life was in his hands. He'd promised he would help her escape. He was her only hope. Tearing at his hair, he dreamt up a plan of sorts, involving guns and shooting their way out. It was madness and Hassan knew it. But it was all he could think of.

CHAPTER ELEVEN
Riding into action

Southern Afghanistan

On the day of the rescue mission, Delta Force dressed in the flowing robes of Baloch tribesmen. They rode at a gallop, making for the meeting with Faruq.

At mid-afternoon they arrived at the entrance to the mountain pass. Connor struggled to rein in his powerful horse. They waited out of the baking sun, scanning the surrounding rocky slopes.

After half an hour, an extremely large man with a long black beard emerged from among the rocks. Men with rifles appeared high up on the mountainside all round Connor and his men. They were surrounded.

"Allah be praised. Major Connor, he is surely the finest horse in all Afghanistan."

Connor dismounted and handed the reins to Faruq. "Yes, and he's all yours."

They greeted formally the Afghan way, embracing and bumping shoulders.

"I thought it best to meet away from my camp, Major," Faruq added. "There are informants everywhere." He waved his men down from the mountainside. "Those you can see are men I know I can trust. We have fought together for many years. Come, we must start our journey to this evening's shura." A look of unease passed across his rugged, weather-beaten face. "I assume you have come to kill the Taliban leader."

"Not exactly," Connor replied.

"Oh?" Faruq looked puzzled.

"He's got something we want."

Faruq frowned.

"Don't worry. As long as you leave by eleven thirty, you'll be safe."

CHAPTER TWELVE
Hassan's gun

Taliban training camp, Afghanistan / Pakistan border

Kate heard the bolt to her cell slide back. Then the door opened and light streamed in.

"I have brought you some bread and water," said Hassan.

"Hurry up, boy," growled one of the guards.

"Listen," Hassan whispered. "I'm not sure how, but I will try and help you to escape. Hold out your hand."

Kate did so and Hassan pressed a pistol into it.

"It's loaded. When the time comes you must be ready to use it."

"But how do we get out of here? There are so many of them. It's suicide, Hassan."

"It may be our only chance."

"No, Hassan.

"No? Then as sure as the sun rises in the east, you will die. It's been decided."

"There's still time for the ransom to be paid."

"The ransom makes no difference. And no one will come to rescue you. No one knows you are here. I will try to get us out. I have to go. May Allah protect us."

CHAPTER THIRTEEN
In the Taliban camp

It had been dark for three hours by the time
Delta Force and Faruq's men reached the valley
of the Taliban camp. Danny and Jacko did a
sweep with night-vision binoculars and thermal-
imaging scopes and located the glow of lookouts
stationed outside the camp's walls. There were
three and they'd be dealt with silently once
Connor was inside.

Connor's men had taken off their Baloch tribal dress to reveal their desert fatigues underneath. They'd also applied black paint to their faces, to camouflage them in the moonlight. Connor was still dressed for the shura. Faruq handed Connor a battered old AK-47. "We leave the horses here. They will expect us all to be armed. But we have to hand in our weapons at the gate and shall have them returned when we leave. No guns are allowed at shuras. Your disguise is acceptable, Major, and your grasp of Pashto sufficient to be understood. But your accent might give you away, so blend in with my men and try to avoid speaking."

"Agreed." Connor slung the rifle over his shoulder. Then he thought twice and handed it back. "I'll be staying when you leave. An extra rifle will raise suspicion. Will they search us?"

Faruq shook his head. "Our customs require a degree of trust on such occasions."

Connor was relieved as he felt safer keeping his combat knife strapped to his left shin.

Faruq led the way with his dozen men, Connor among them, along the stony path towards the glow of lamps and the gate to the Taliban's fortified compound. A face appeared over the parapet and called out. Faruq responded. As they

waited for the gates to open, Connor leaned
forward and whispered, "Remember, Faruq,
make damn sure you and your men are out of
there by eleven thirty. And, whatever you do,
don't head north or else you might run into a
rather nasty surprise."

Once inside and disarmed, the party were led
towards a large, two-storey building. Meanwhile,
outside, Sparks remained at the evac co-ordinates.
He maintained radio contact with CENTCOM and
the rest of Delta Force. Jacko sloped off into the
night, a silencer attached to his M4 rifle, and
Sam followed. Within the hour they had dealt
with the external lookouts.

Danny and Ben had the hardest job of all.
Carrying the heavy blanket explosive in
camouflaged backpacks they crawled lizard-like,
chins in the dirt, slowly towards the south-west
corner of the training camp. Progress was
painfully slow with long spells lying perfectly
still in the moon shadows.

Drawing closer, they could hear voices and saw
that the Taliban had posted guards on the walls
and roof of the tower. Still they pressed on and,
reaching the wall, slipped off their backpacks.
They primed the charges and placed them in
position. They were about to retreat when a

sudden scuffle from the parapet above made them freeze. Someone peered down towards where they lay. Ben held his breath. Had they been heard? Gently, he reached to his belt for his Glock handgun. The face eventually vanished but before either Danny or Ben could breathe a sigh of relief, a naked backside appeared instead. And then they heard splattering and the air filled with a stink. They didn't wait for the man to finish before retreating to the cover of some boulders.

*   *   *   *   *   *

Faruq and his men settled down on some plump cushions. They faced the Taliban's representatives across the room. Connor studied the camp's leader, a man finely dressed with a golden hat made from karakul skins, and gold rings on his fingers. To his left was the camp's mullah, and to his right was a man with his arm in a sling; Masud. Connor recognised him from intel he'd studied.

A succession of food on trays was brought in and the feast began; spicy meat dishes, roasted corn, nuts and gallons of sweet tea. Conversation was polite and trivial. Connor had to bide his time. It was too early to act.

With the feasting over, talk turned to the business of stolen chickens, appropriate compensation, and a string of promises. Connor could tell the Taliban leader cared little for the Baloch, and he sensed Faruq felt the same about the Taliban.

Beneath his turban, Connor was wearing a covert earpiece. He heard Sparks updating the team. "Arrow and Spear are in position. Helos are on their way and on schedule for the evac. Code Green. We have clearance to proceed. Check your weapons and detonate charges at zero hour when Arrow set off their flares. Good luck."

The shura drew to a close shortly before eleven fifteen. Everyone headed outside via a narrow corridor. Connor knew it was time to make his move. He dipped through an open side door leading to a storeroom. Feeling his way through the dark to the window, he gently forced it open and climbed out. A nearby rainwater tank offered cover. As Faruq's party exited through the gate, Connor took stock of his surroundings.

There were Taliban guards everywhere. Connor could see the tower in which Kate Shawcross was hopefully still being held on the far side of the camp. First, though, he needed to locate Hassan. There were numerous buildings to check out, some lit by oil lamps and all hives of activity. In one, men knelt and prayed. In another a dozen or so were reading aloud from the Qur'an. In a third building ten more Taliban were cleaning their rifles.

Connor cursed under his breath. "Where the hell are you, Hassan?" It was twenty to twelve. He realised he had little choice other than ask around. Spotting a tall man crossing the camp, Connor set off after him.

"I'm looking for Hassan," Connor said.

"What do you want with the boy?" Amin asked. "And who are you? I don't recognise you."

Sensing he was about to raise the alarm, Connor pulled the man into the shadows. He gripped the man's throat. "Where's the boy? I won't ask again."

"I'm here. Now leave my friend alone," said Hassan as he pointed an AK-47 at Connor.

CHAPTER FOURTEEN
Connor finds Hassan

"He's an infidel imposter, Hassan. Shoot him. Shoot him now," Amin demanded.

"Be quiet." Connor tightened his choking grip. "Listen, Hassan. I know who you are. I'm an old friend of your father's. I've come to rescue you and Miss Shawcross."

The rifle shook in Hassan's hands. "Liar. Let my friend go."

"My name's Nathan Connor. I knew your father as a boy. I blame myself that the Taliban came and killed your family, Hassan. I promised him I'd look after you."

"The *Taliban* killed your family?" Amin repeated in surprise. "Hassan, you never said..."

Hassan lowered his rifle. "I remember you. You came to my village."

"Yes. Yes, Hassan. And I promised your father that if anything happened to him I'd find you and help you. I've been searching for you for weeks. Listen, we haven't got much time. We must get to Miss Shawcross."

"Don't listen to him, Hassan," Amin spluttered.

"Come with us, Amin. You don't belong here.

Most of these men aren't even Afghans. And all they want to do is kill people."

"No. Never. Shoot him, Hass—"

Connor twisted Amin's head. He went limp and slipped from Connor's grip. "Sorry, Hassan, but there's no time for lengthy discussions."

"You killed my friend!"

"No, Hassan, just rendered him unconscious. Now, we must get to Miss Shawcross."

Together they headed for the tower. "She is in a room on the first floor. The door is bolted and there are two guards. I visited her earlier and gave her a gun."

Connor stopped abruptly. "You did what?"

"They were going to kill her, ransom or no ransom. That is wrong. I was going to help her escape. That's why I have this rifle."

"Jesus!" Hassan's courage, and stupidity, had taken Connor by surprise.

Reaching the entrance to the tower, Connor whispered, "At midnight we're going to blast the wall in order to create a way out. All hell will break loose. I need you to remain calm and do exactly as I say. Now, give me that rifle. Go up the stairs first and distract the guards. I'll deal with them." Kneeling down, he removed his combat knife. Hassan gawped at it.

CHAPTER FIFTEEN
Zero hour

Kate heard a scuffle outside. She held out her pistol, pointing it unsteadily towards the door.

The door burst open and Hassan stood before her. "You must lie down, Kate. Now!"

"What?"

Connor came into view holding his blood-covered knife. "I'm Major Connor. Please, miss, do exactly what Hassan says."

Flares arced into the sky and cast a flickering white light over the camp. The first mortar shells screamed in from the north and exploded in the compound, just as Danny detonated the blanket charges.

The tower shuddered. A huge crack appeared in the wall and debris showered down from the ceiling onto Connor's head. He leaped to his feet and dragged a bewildered Kate through the swirling cloud of dust towards the door. "Hassan, you all right?"

Coughing and spluttering, Hassan replied, "Yes, sir."

Together they hurried down the stairs into the courtyard. Buildings to the north were on fire and Taliban fighters were running to defend the camp. Others were already firing their rifles into the night from positions on top of the wall. "This way," Connor yelled, heading for the blast hole in the wall, with Kate and Hassan close behind.

Connor shot two Taliban who blocked their path. Then two more fighters on the wall turned to shoot. Connor took out one, but the other had a clear shot. Then suddenly the man collapsed, and toppled down into the courtyard. Connor had Sam Wilson to thank for that later.

Danny and Ben emerged from the hole in the wall and adopted crouching positions. "Got you covered, sir," Danny shouted.

Connor guided Kate and Hassan as they clambered over the pile of rubble and through the hole. Jacko and Sam were waiting further up the valley. "Sir," Jacko called out. He waved them forward. "This way to our helo. She's just touched down but won't want to hang around."

CHAPTER SIXTEEN
Helicopter evac

Their helo took to the air under full power and banked steeply. Kate couldn't stop shaking. "You came. I didn't think you would. I'd given up hope."

"Sorry we took so long, miss," Connor replied.

Hassan had only ever seen helicopters flying overhead. He'd certainly never flown in one, but he was glad to be out of Masud's reach and away from the Taliban. Sparks leaned forward and grabbed his shoulder. He shouted over the noise of the helo, "Major Connor risked his career, not to mention his life, to find and rescue you."

"My father was his best friend. He was always talking about him. Thank you for rescuing us. Our prayers were answered. *Allahu Akbar*, sir, *Allahu Akbar*. God is greatest!"

Sparks smiled and slapped his shoulder.

Bright light suddenly bathed the interior of the helicopter and moments later it rocked gently as the pressure waves struck it. "Don't look so alarmed, miss," Danny called out to Kate. "It's the air strike. By the time they're done, there'll be nothing but dust down there."

Hassan pressed his face against one of the small windows as he suddenly remembered Amin.

Hassan knew they were both on different paths, but perhaps with time Amin would have seen how senseless it all was. He slumped back down, drew his knees up to his chin and buried his head. He was alone in the world again, with no father or mother, and no friends. But at least he still had someone looking over him.

Connor stared at Hassan with a huge feeling of relief. Somehow, they'd all got out alive. Perhaps his nightmares would go now.

He rested his head back and closed his weary eyes. "I've kept my promise to you, Assif, old friend. I have found Hassan, your son," he muttered. But Connor realised he hadn't thought any further than that. He puffed out his cheeks and sighed. He'd do what he could for the boy. But in the most dangerous, lawless, poverty-stricken place on Earth, how would Hassan ever be safe?

Connor could hear his men celebrating. The mission had been a success. And that's how they had to live, from one moment to the next. Who knows what tomorrow would hold? But for now, they were alive, and that was enough.

WEAPONS and GEAR

M4 CARBINE (5.56MM)
with Delta Force accessories

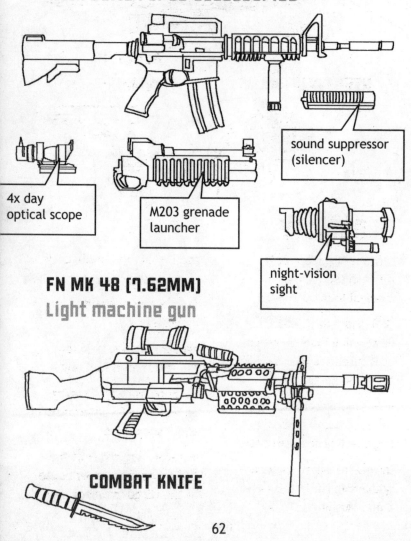

sound suppressor
(silencer)

4x day
optical scope

M203 grenade
launcher

night-vision
sight

FN MK 48 (7.62MM)
Light machine gun

COMBAT KNIFE

M110A1 [7.62MM]
Semi-automatic sniper system

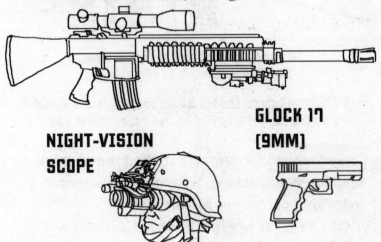

NIGHT-VISION SCOPE

GLOCK 17 [9MM]

GLOSSARY

fentanyl lollipop pain relief in the form of a medical lollipop

GPS short for Global Positioning System, which uses satellites to track things on Earth

IEDs Improvised Explosive Devices, home-made bombs triggered by remote control

infidel refers to someone without faith, in this case, a non-Muslim

intel short for intelligence

polio a disease which affects muscles and movement

ransom money paid for the return of something

reconnaissance scouting or searching for information about something

senator a member of the US Senate, the upper house of the US government

63

More explosive action in Book 3, when the Taliban launch a deadly attack.

Major Nathan Connor and his Delta Force team are assigned to strike back at a Taliban leader called Mullah Khan.

Connor leaned forward and studied the photo of a plump, bearded man, wearing a black turban and with a patch over his left eye.

"Do we know where and when the meet will take place, sir?"

"No. If we did there'd be no need for me to be talking to you, Major. Instead, I'd be arranging an air strike." Rogers returned to the map of the Hindu Kush Mountains and pointed vaguely. "Most likely, they'll get together somewhere around here. There are lots of old silver mines. Perfect for hiding out."

"Let me get this straight, sir," Connor interrupted. "You want us to locate this Mullah Khan and find out when and where the meeting will take place, so you can then arrange a targeted air strike."

Colonel Rogers nodded. "Got it in one, Major."

Continued in: Task Force Delta — First Strike